Please & Thank You

Your Guide to Becoming the Perfect Princess!

White Plains, New York • Montréal, Québec • Bath, United Kingdom

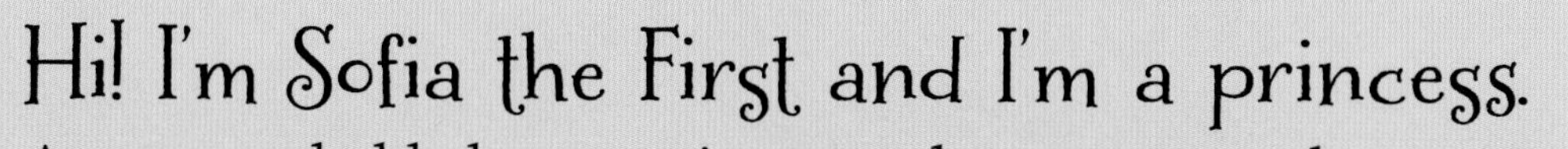

As you probably know, princesses have very good manners. I haven't always been a princess, so I have had a lot to learn.

With the help of my family and friends, I have learned some great lessons along the way. I can't wait to share my story with you and then you can share your story with me!

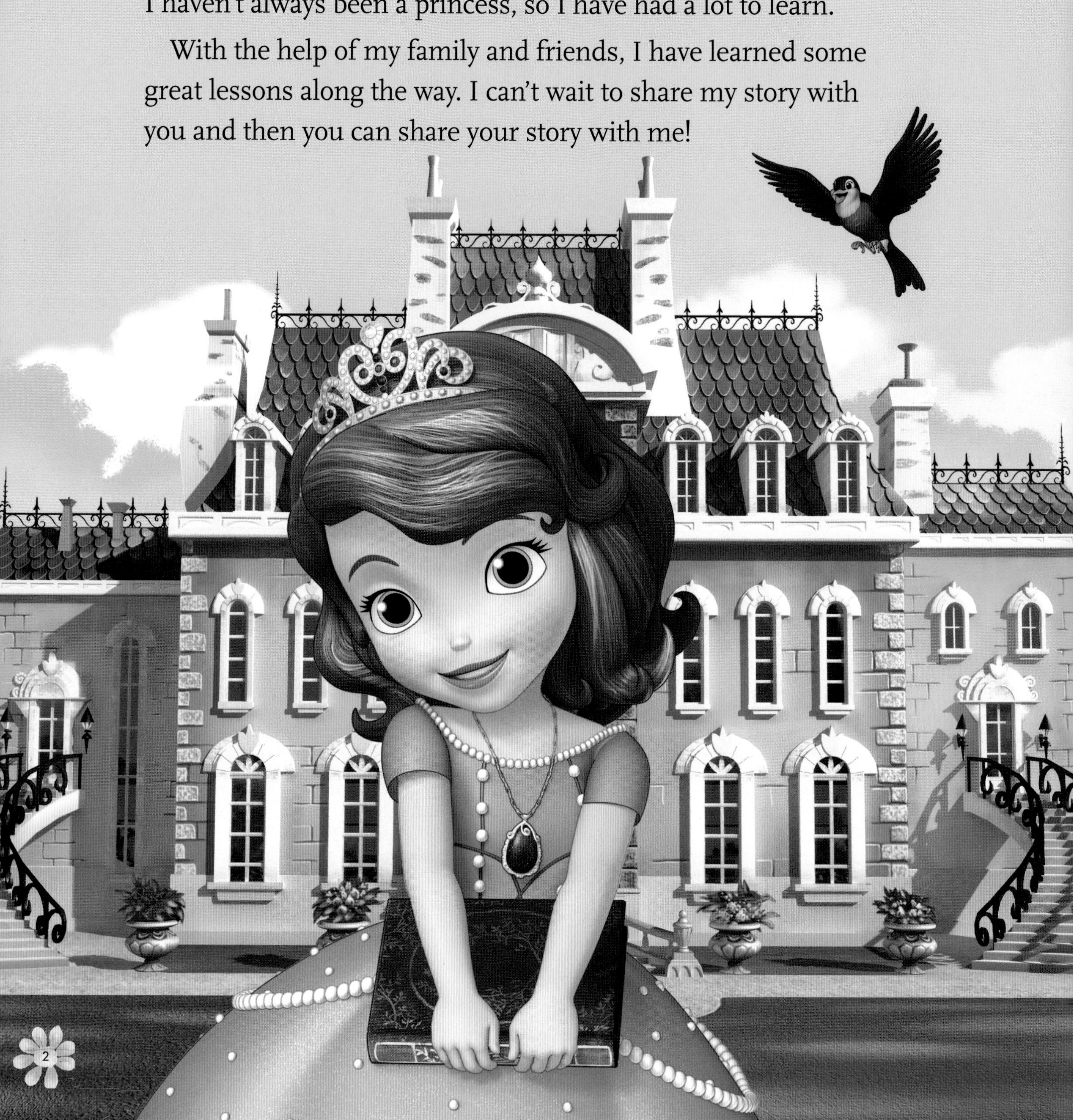

At Royal Prep we learn a lot about manners. Today's lesson is about the proper way to pour tea. I try and I try, but I still make a mess. Miss Flora tells me to keep practicing. She will test me again next week. "Thank you!" I tell her.

Sometimes I worry that I'll never learn everything about being a proper princess. It seems like everyone knows more than I do. If I am going to be the best princess I can be, I am going to need some help.

James has very good manners. He pours tea for me and my friends before he helps himself. "Please, will you help me learn proper manners?" I ask him. James is happy to show me everything he knows.

James also helps me with my table manners. I can never remember which fork I am supposed to use! He reminds me to put my napkin on my lap and explains that I should wait for my turn to talk at the table.

"Thank you!" I tell him.

And he says, "You're welcome!"

A proper princess knows how to dance. “Please, will you help me practice?” I ask Amber. Amber teaches me what she knows. She reminds me to say “Excuse me” if I bump into someone.

She even shows me how to curtsy.

“Thank you!” I tell her.

“You’re welcome,” Amber says.

King Roland knows that there is a lot for me to learn.

He reminds me that I don't have to learn all my manners at once.

"Just do your best," he tells me.

I want to learn to be a proper princess, but sometimes I just want to be myself and have fun. So I gather all of my animal friends for a picnic.

"Thank you, Sofia!" they cheer.

"You're welcome," I tell them!

And now it's time for you to tell me all about you!

Use this book to fill in what you know and what you want to learn. You will have princess manners in no time!

My Manners Book

A book about me!

My name is:

____

Put your photo here.

When I was a baby, my parents had to do everything for me, but now that I am ______ years old, I can do all kinds of things by myself.

Here are some things I can do all by myself:

- Feed my pet ☐
- Set the table ☐
- Clear the table ☐
- Make my bed ☐
- Brush my teeth ☐
- Get dressed ☐
- Put my toys away ☐
- Tie my shoes ☐
- Sweep the floor ☐

Sofia is learning how to have princess manners.

© Disney
© Disney
© Disney
© Disney
Magical
© Disney
Thank You
© Disney
© Disney
© Disney
© Disney
© Disney
© Disney
© Disney
© Disney
© Disney
© Disney
© Disney
© Disney
© Disney
Thank You
© Disney
© Disney
© Disney
© Disney
© Disney
PERFECT!
© Disney
© Disney
© Disney
© Disney
© Disney
© Disney
© Disney
© Disney
© Disney
© Disney
© Disney
© Disney
© Disney
© Disney
© Disney
ROYAL JOB!
© Disney
© Disney
© Disney
© Disney
© Disney
© Disney

Please
Magical
ROYAL JOB!
Thank You
Magical
PERFECT!

I am working on my manners, too!
These are some things I know I should do:

I say "Please"
when I ask for something.

I say "Thank you" when someone
does something nice for me.

When someone offers me something
I don't want, I say "No, thank you."

When someone thanks me,
I say "You're welcome."

I am happy to share my toys.

When I need something from someone
who is busy, I say "Excuse Me."

I also say "Excuse Me"
when I bump into someone.

When a door is closed, I knock before I go in.

Learning good manners takes lots of practice!

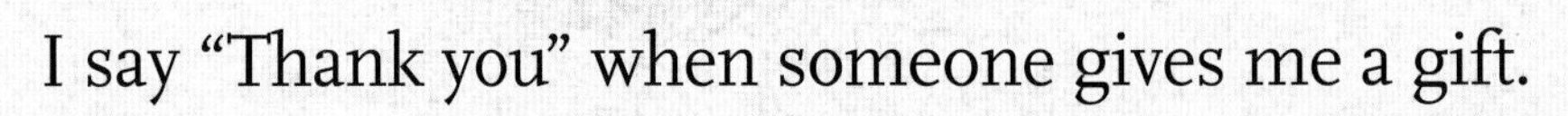

I say "Thank you" when someone gives me a gift.

This is a picture of the best gift I ever got.

Draw a picture here.

I say “Nice to meet you” when I meet someone new.

This is the name of someone I met this year.

Sofia is learning to have good manners at the royal table.

I am learning good table manners, too!

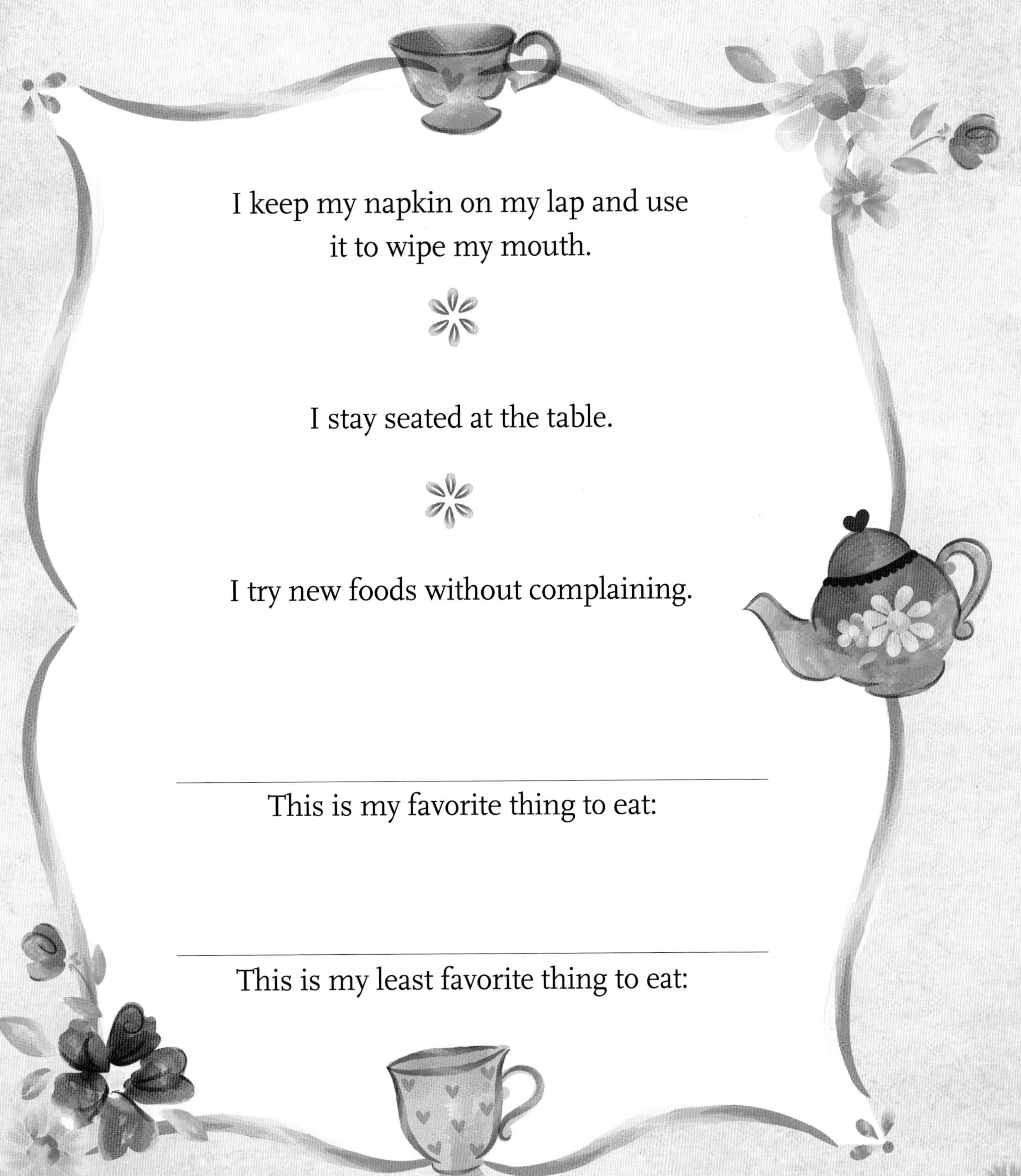

I keep my napkin on my lap and use it to wipe my mouth.

I stay seated at the table.

I try new foods without complaining.

This is my favorite thing to eat:

This is my least favorite thing to eat:

I know that it is important to help whenever I can!

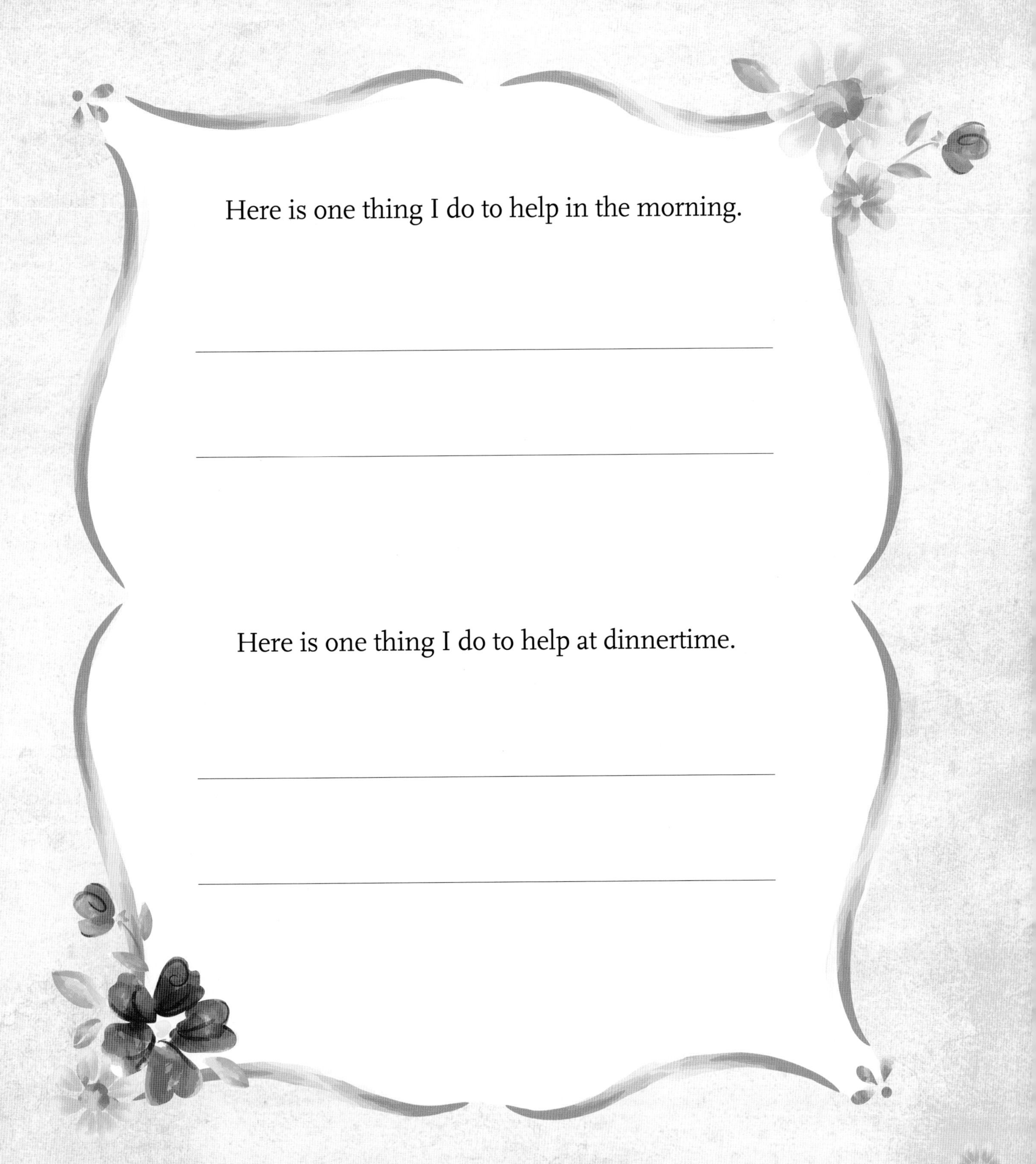

Here is one thing I do to help in the morning.

Here is one thing I do to help at dinnertime.

Here is one thing I can do to help a friend.

Well, that's it! This is my book about me.
Sofia and I always try to be the best we can be!

Here is one thing I can do to help someone in my family.

	Sticker Goal	Stickers Earned
Week 1		
Week 2		
Week 3		
Week 4		

Princess

FRIDAY	SATURDAY	SUNDAY

Learning to Be a P

ONDAY	TUESDAY	WEDNESDAY	THURSDAY

Helping your child practice manners is simple with this chart!

Fill in some of the manners that you and your child are practicing. Each time your child is successful with that task, she can put a sticker on the correct day on the chart. Decide how many stickers you hope your child will earn each week. Count up the stickers at the end of the week and see if your child earns a reward.

The stickers are removable so you can use them again and again.

Place a photo of your child here.

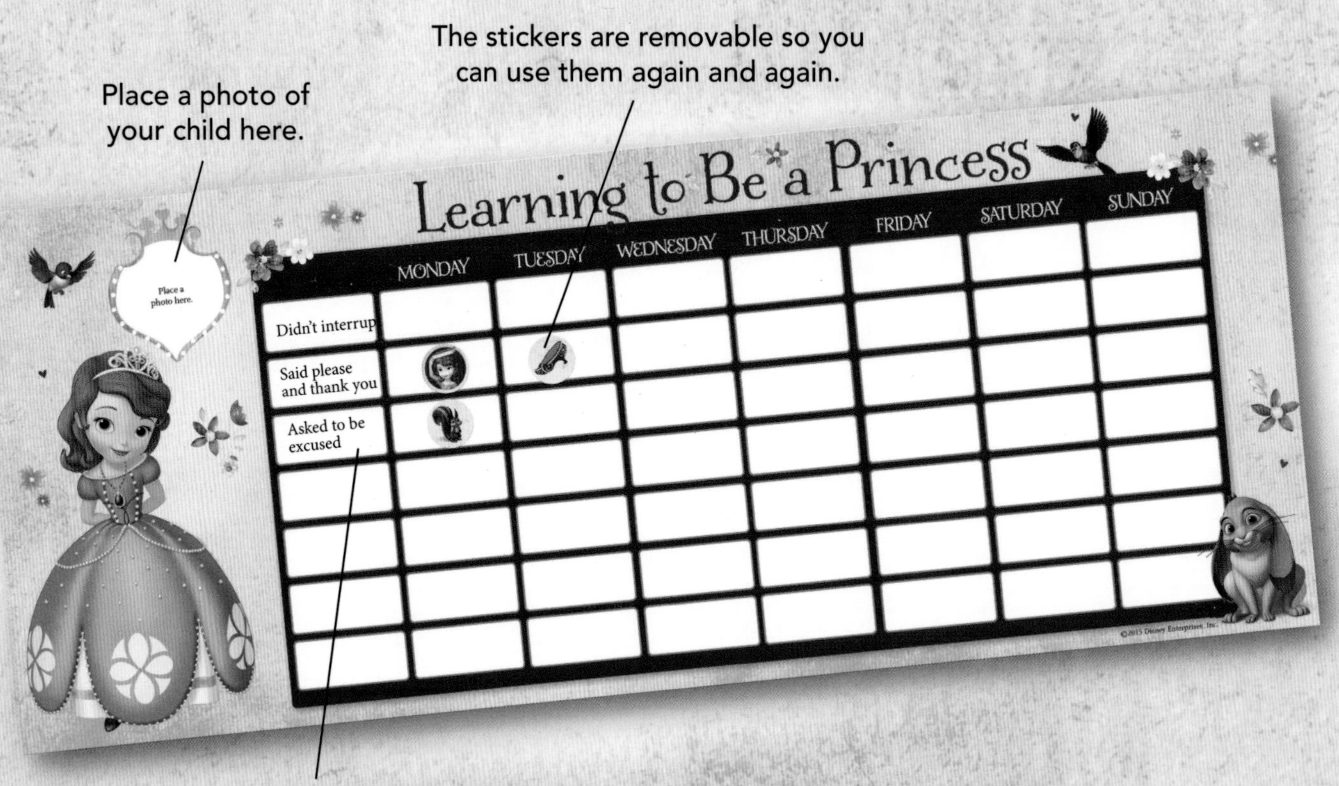

Fill in your own manners here.

Place a
photo here.
M